DETECTING DISASTERS

DETECTING HURRICANES

by Samantha S. Bell

I0892611

FOCUS READERS

North Star Editions

WWW.NORTHSTAREDITIONS.COM

Copyright © 2017 by North Star Editions, Lake Elmo, MN 55042. All rights reserved. No part of this book may be reproduced or utilized in any form or by any means without written permission from the publisher.

Produced for North Star Editions by Red Line Editorial.

Photographs ©: Mike Groll/AP Images, cover, 1, 7; NOAA, 4–5, 17, 19, 23; Chieh Cheng/iStockphoto, 8–9; Kevork Djansezian/AP Images, 13; Universal History Archive/UIG/Getty Images, 14–15; Chris Sattlberger/Science Source, 20–21; Red Line Editorial, 25; J Pat Carter/AP Images, 26–27

Content Consultant: Jim Lawrence, Adjunct Professor of Earth and Atmospheric Sciences, University of Houston

ISBN
978-1-63517-003-0 (hardcover)
978-1-63517-059-7 (paperback)
978-1-63517-165-5 (ebook pdf)
978-1-63517-115-0 (hosted ebook)

Library of Congress Control Number: 2016949764

Printed in the United States of America
Mankato, MN
September, 2018

ABOUT THE AUTHOR

Samantha Bell lives with her family and lots of pets in the foothills of South Carolina. She loves writing about nature, and she is the author or illustrator of more than 60 books for children.

TABLE OF CONTENTS

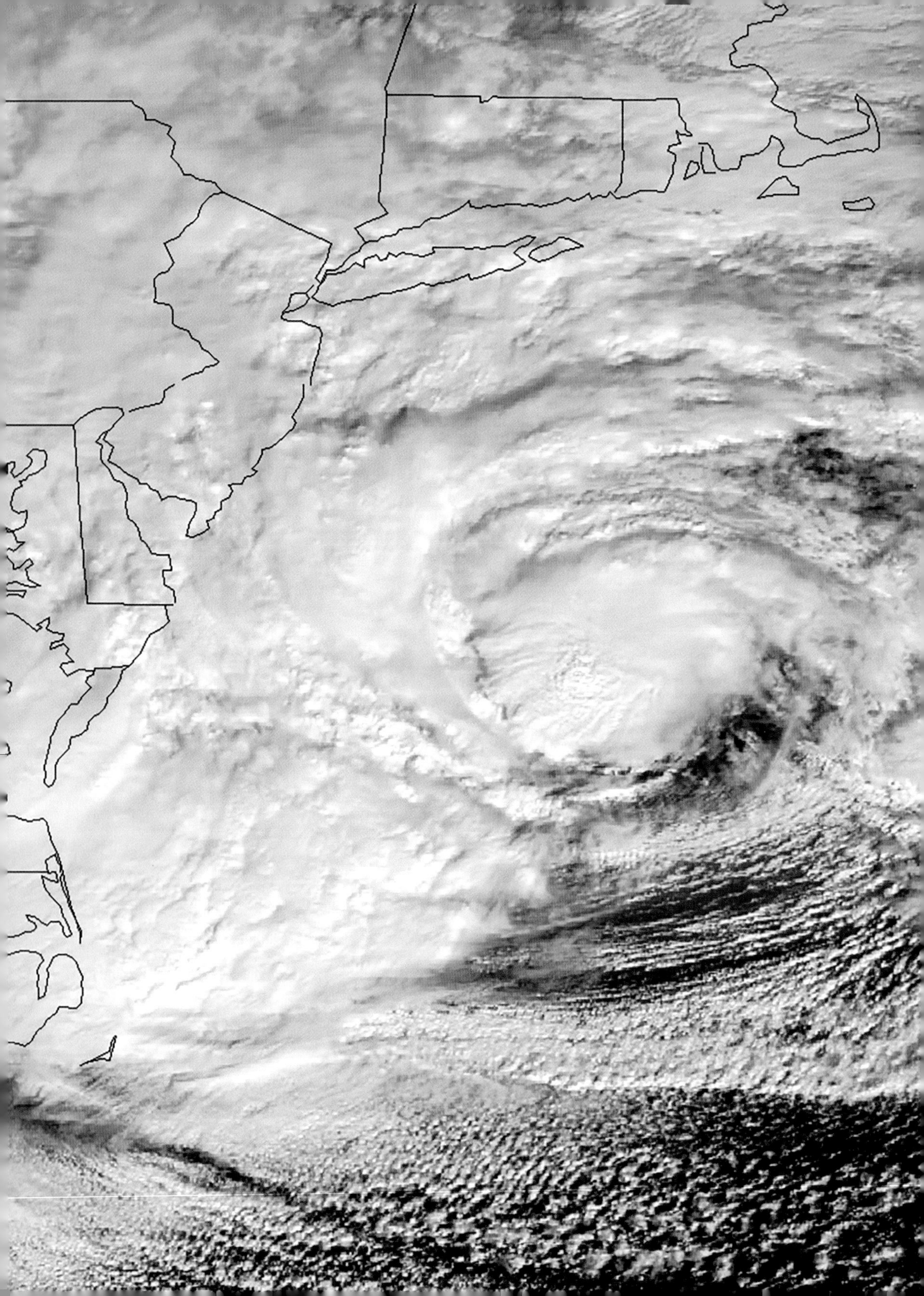

CHAPTER 1

HURRICANE SANDY

On the morning of October 29, 2012, the National Hurricane Center gave the official report. The winds from Hurricane Sandy were approaching the coastlines of New Jersey, Delaware, and Virginia. People in the path of the deadly storm headed for shelter as the wind and rain began beating down.

Hurricane Sandy headed for the US coastline in late October 2012.

Sandy's fierce winds pushed water from the Atlantic Ocean to the shore. They also caused blizzard conditions in the mountains of Maryland and West Virginia.

During the hurricane, a **storm surge** pounded the coastline. Major cities were flooded, and bridges were closed. Millions

FORECASTING HURRICANES

There are three types of hurricane predictions. The first involves the likelihood a hurricane will form. Scientists predict the number of storms in a season based on past storms and the **climate**. The second type of prediction involves hurricanes that have already formed. Scientists try to predict the paths the storms will take. The third involves how a hurricane's strength changes over time.

Sandy devastated homes and other buildings on the New Jersey coastline.

of people lost power. Seventy-two people in the United States died, along with dozens of people in the Caribbean. But it could have been even worse if the residents had not been warned. Scientists use many methods to detect and follow hurricanes. Their early warnings save lives.

CHAPTER 2

WHAT IS A HURRICANE?

A hurricane is a type of tropical cyclone, which is a large swirling storm with strong winds. To form, it needs warm water and warm air. The water must be at least 80 degrees Fahrenheit (27°C).

Hurricanes start to form when the warm, moist air above the ocean's surface rises. More air moves into its place.

Hurricanes pick up energy from warm waters, leading to strong winds and fierce rainfall.

Then this new air becomes warm and moist, and it rises as well. When it rises high enough, the air cools off and starts to form columns of cumulus clouds. The air begins to spin, and the wind moves faster and faster around the center of the columns. Wind carries the storm across the ocean. The storm becomes even stronger as it moves over more warm water.

Storms with winds blowing at less than 39 miles per hour (63 km/h) are called tropical depressions. But the winds can pick up speed. If they blow from 39 to 73 miles per hour (63 to 118 km/h), the storm is called a tropical storm. When the winds reach speeds of 74 miles per hour (119 km/h) or higher, the storm has become a hurricane.

HOW STRONG IS THE STORM?

Hurricane Category	Wind Speeds
Category 1	74–95 miles per hour (119–153 km/h)
Category 2	96–110 miles per hour (154–177 km/h)
Category 3	111–129 miles per hour (178–208 km/h)
Category 4	130–156 miles per hour (209–251 km/h)
Category 5	157+ miles per hour (252+ km/h)

Hurricanes can be 400 to 500 miles (640 to 800 km) across and more than 50,000 feet (15,240 m) high. The center of the storm, called the eye, can be 12 to 30 miles (19 to 48 km) wide. A ring of cumulus clouds swirls around the eye, forming the eye wall. The harshest winds and heaviest rains are found here. Less severe clouds and rain extend far from the eye wall.

If a hurricane reaches land, it pushes a wall of ocean water ashore. This storm surge, combined with heavy rains, can cause massive flooding and damage. Hurricane Katrina's storm surge in 2005 was 28 feet (8.5 m) high. In 2008,

Storm surges can be powerful enough to carry away cars.

Hurricane Ike had a storm surge that was 20 feet (6.1 m) high and moved more than 30 miles (48 km) inland.

CHAPTER 3

INTO THE STORM

Because a hurricane can cause a lot of damage and even loss of life, it is important that people know it is coming. That way, they can prepare for the storm. But for many years, warning systems did not give people much time.

Hurricanes were once reported by people on ships and tropical islands.

Before the 1900s, people had little warning before hurricanes struck land.

In the early 1900s, planes would set out to observe the weather and send in updates. They estimated wind speeds and direction based on the ocean's waves.

Then, in 1943, Lieutenant Colonel Joseph Duckworth took a plane directly into a hurricane. He was trying to prove that the plane was strong. But his actions also showed that planes could be used to study and track storms. Scientists could get more accurate estimates of a storm's position and intensity. After a hurricane hit Miami, Florida, in 1945, the US military created the Hurricane Hunters squadron. The squadron's aircraft and crews still fly into hurricanes today.

Today's Hurricane Hunters fly large WC-130 aircraft into storms.

In the 1950s, Hurricanes Carol, Edna, Hazel, and Diane hit the United States. Together, they caused more than $1.5 billion in damage. Because of these storms, the US Weather Bureau started sending research flights into hurricanes.

After Diane, the US Weather Bureau and the military joined together to use computers to forecast the weather.

The United States launched its first weather **satellite** in 1960. It could take

NAMING HURRICANES

Until the early 1950s, hurricanes were identified by the year and order in which they occurred. But this caused confusion when two or more storms made **landfall** at the same time. So in 1953, the United States began using female names. By 1979, both male and female names were used. For Atlantic hurricanes, most names are reused every six years. If a storm is very costly or deadly, its name is not used again. Sandy and Katrina are among the retired names.

Weather satellites help scientists make hurricane predictions more accurate.

pictures of hurricanes from space. As technology continued to improve, so did the satellites. Today, satellites measure cloud and ocean temperatures, how fast rain falls, and how tall the clouds are. Scientists use all of this data to understand how hurricanes form. The data also helps them predict the strength of the hurricane and the path it will take.

CAUTION

CHAPTER 4

GOING HIGHER-TECH

As technology improves, so do the instruments scientists use to study hurricanes. The more scientists know about a storm, the better they can understand it.

In the 1970s, two WP-3D Orion aircraft were built for research. They remained in use for several decades.

In the air and on the ground, scientists use technology to learn more about hurricanes.

By 2016, the planes had more scientific instruments, **radars**, and recording systems than ever before.

In 1982, the Hurricane Hunters used **dropsondes** for the first time. Planes dropped the instruments into Hurricane Debby as it moved over the ocean. On the way down, the dropsondes measured the temperature, pressure, winds, and humidity.

Scientists also use unmanned aerial vehicles (UAVs) to gather information. These remote-controlled planes can fly lower than regular planes. Scientists fly them into storms, collect data, and then fly them out again. In 2006, scientists

Drones can be much smaller and nimbler than piloted aircraft.

decided to fly a UAV into Tropical Storm Ophelia until the fuel ran out. They did it again in 2007 with Hurricane Noel. Although the UAVs were lost, scientists were able to gather valuable information about the storms.

DROPSONDE

A dropsonde is a package of instruments in a tube with a parachute on top. When the dropsonde is dropped from a plane, the parachute keeps it from falling too fast. On the way down, dropsondes take measurements every half second and send the information to the plane.

Each dropsonde is about the size of a cardboard tube inside a paper towel roll.

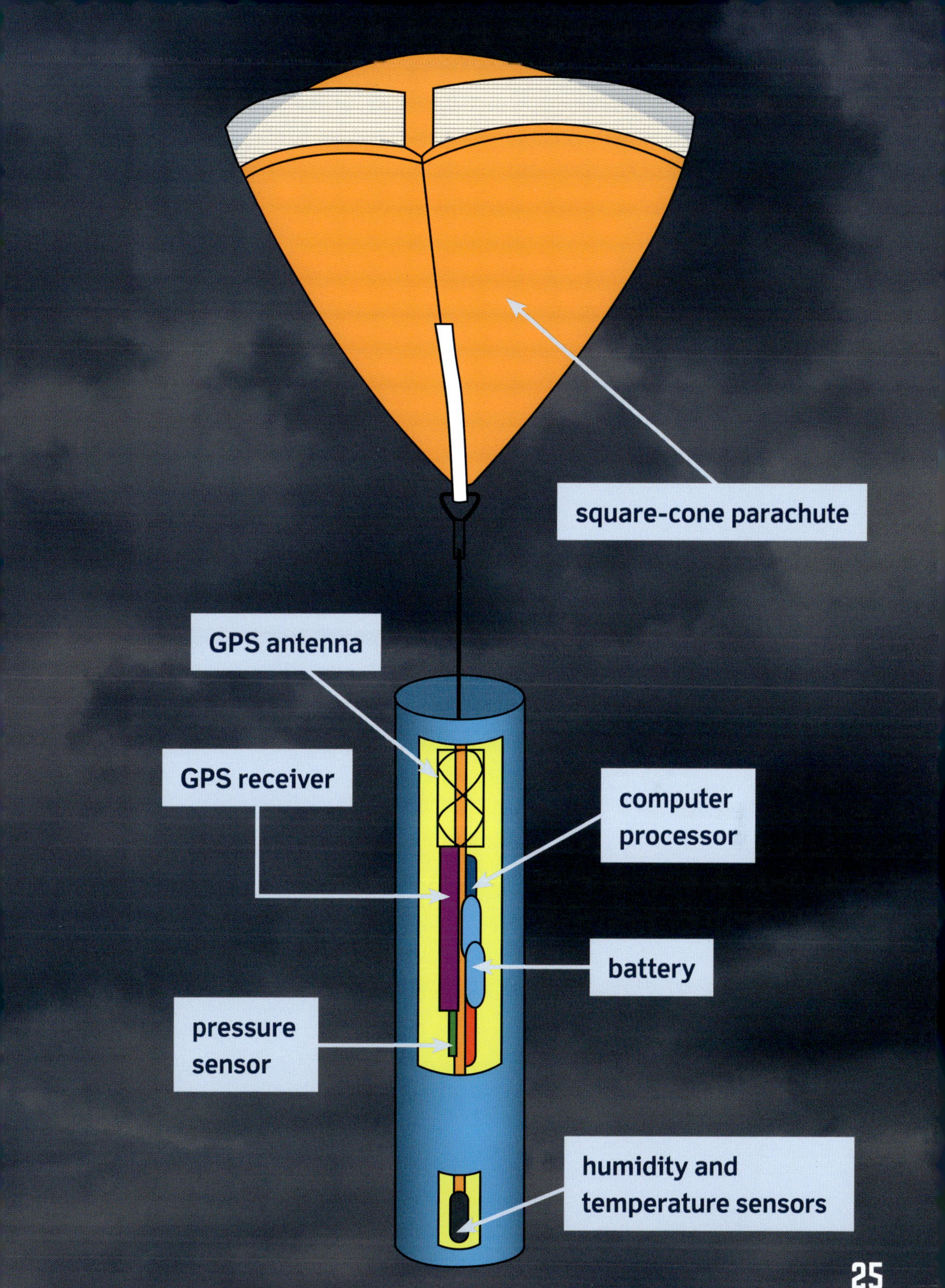
square-cone parachute
GPS antenna
GPS receiver
computer processor
battery
pressure sensor
humidity and temperature sensors

CHAPTER 5

READY FOR THE NEXT STORM

The Atlantic hurricane season runs from June 1 to November 30. The Eastern Pacific hurricane season runs from May 15 to November 30. So every spring, **meteorologists** start giving the public estimates of how many storms there may be and how many are expected to make landfall.

Meteorologists are always watching for storms that could threaten the United States.

The National Hurricane Center is responsible for forecasting all tropical cyclones around North America. It uses computers to make predictions with the information it receives from aircraft, satellites, and radar.

Predicting a storm's path and intensity helps people prepare for it. Sometimes residents need to **evacuate**. The sooner people are warned, the more time they have to take action.

Hurricanes are huge, dangerous storms. The better we understand them, the more people we can keep safe. By making accurate hurricane predictions, scientists help save many lives every year.

HURRICANE SAFETY CHECKLIST

- Trim damaged trees and secure loose rain gutters.
- Bring loose objects inside.
- Cover all of your home's windows with either storm shutters or plywood cut to fit.
- Make a disaster supply kit with a flashlight, batteries, first aid supplies, and cash.
- Know where to go if you have to evacuate. Know the route to take and where you can stay.
- If your area will not be evacuated, buy enough supplies for several days in case you lose power and water.
- Make a family emergency communication plan. Charge your cell phone in case you lose power.
- Turn your refrigerator or freezer to the coldest setting. If you lose power, food will last longer.
- Check your television, your radio, or the Internet for weather updates and emergency instructions.

FOCUS ON

DETECTING HURRICANES

Write your answers on a separate piece of paper.

1. Summarize Chapter 3 of this book.
2. Do you agree that hurricanes should have people's names rather than numbers, years, or other kinds of names? Why or why not?
3. Which devices do scientists drop into hurricanes to take measurements?
   - A. satellites
   - B. dropsondes
   - C. buoys
4. What category of hurricane causes the most damage?
   - A. Category 1
   - B. Category 3
   - C. Category 5

Answer key on page 32.

GLOSSARY

climate
The average weather conditions of a particular place or region.

dropsondes
Packages of instruments dropped from a plane to gather information about a storm.

evacuate
To leave a place of danger.

landfall
Arrival on a coastline.

meteorologists
Scientists who study the weather.

radars
Devices that send out radio waves for detecting and locating objects.

satellite
An object or vehicle that orbits Earth, the moon, or another body in space.

storm surge
A rising of the sea as a result of the wind associated with a storm.

TO LEARN MORE

BOOKS

Benoit, Peter. *Hurricane Katrina*. New York: Scholastic, 2011.

Challoner, Jack. *Hurricane and Tornado*. New York: DK Books, 2014.

Gregory, Josh. *The Superstorm Hurricane Sandy*. New York: Scholastic, 2013.

Kostigen, Thomas. *Extreme Weather: Surviving Tornadoes, Sandstorms, Hailstorms, Blizzards, Hurricanes, and More!* Washington, DC: National Geographic Children's Books, 2014.

NOTE TO EDUCATORS

Visit **www.focusreaders.com** to find lesson plans, activities, links, and other resources related to this title.

INDEX

Answer Key: 1. Answers will vary; **2.** Answers will vary; **3.** B; **4.** C